DATE DUE

DEC 1 2 2005	
JAN 2 6 2006	
MAR 1 3 2006	
APR 2 1 2006	

GAYLORD   PRINTED IN U.S.A.

K

P

G

X

APE
IN A
CAPE

APE IN A

an alphabet of odd animals

CAPE

by Fritz Eichenberg

Voyager Books • Harcourt, Inc.

San Diego   New York   London

www.HarcourtBooks.com

Voyager Books is a trademark of Harcourt, Inc., registered
in the United States of American and/or other jurisdictions.

The Library of Congress has cataloged the hardcover edition as follows:
Eichenberg, Fritz, 1901–1990
Ape in a cape: an alphabet of odd animals/Fritz Eichenberg.
p. cm.
Summary: An assortment of animals introduces letters of the alphabet.
[1. Alphabet. 2. Animals—Pictorial works.] I. Title.
PZ7.E343Ap 1952
[E]—dc19 52-6908
ISBN 0-15-203722-5
ISBN 0-15-607830-9 pb

N P R S Q O

Manufactured by South China Printing Company, Ltd., China

A

Ape in a cape

Bear in despair

Carp with a harp

D

Dove in love

E Egret in a minuet

Fox in a box

Goat in a boat

Hare at the fair

Irish setter with a letter

Jay in May

Kitten with a mitten

Lizard with a wizard

Mouse in a blouse

Nag with a bag

Owl on the prowl

Pig in a wig

TRAIL

Q

Quail on the trail

R

Rat with a bat

Sheep in a leap

T

Toad on the road

U Unicorn with a horn

Vulture with culture

Whale in a gale

X for Rex

Y

Yak with a pack

Z for zoo

H

F

U

B

K

P

G

X